THISTLE

Thistle

A Story of Ghosts, Memories & Ashes

by Emily Capettini

Cover Photo © Copyright Corbis/42-30533422 Thistle head

Cover text set in Lithos Pro & Kabel Lt. Std
Interior text set in Adobe Garamond Pro, Lithos Pro & Kabel Lt. Std.

Cover and Interior Design by Ken Keegan

Offset printed in the United States
by Edwards Brothers Malloy, Ann Arbor, Michigan
On 55# Heritage Book Cream White Antique
Acid Free Archival Quality Recycled Paper
with Rainbow FSC Certified Colored End Papers

Library of Congress Cataloging-in-Publication Data

Capettini, Emily, 1987-
  Thistle : a story of ghosts, memories, & ashes / Emily Capettini.
  pages cm
  ISBN 978-1-63243-014-4 (pbk. : alk. paper)
  1. Mothers and daughters--Fiction. 2. Mothers--Death--Fiction.
  3. Grief--Fiction 4. Self-actualization (Psychology)--Fiction.
  5. Psychological fiction. I. Title.
PS3603.A6665T55 2015
813'.6--dc23
                                        2015023280

Published by Omnidawn Publishing, Richmond, California
www.omnidawn.com (510) 237-5472   (800) 792-4957
              10 9 8 7 6 5 4 3 2 1
              ISBN: 978-1-63243-014-4

1

She's in the kitchen, on her toes to reach the tea in the top cabinet, when Minerva sees her mother at the edge of her vision, hovering near a cracked, stained teacup on a cold March morning. She flickers like the old fluorescent bulb that had hung in her mother's cellar.

Her mother's lips stretch soundlessly. Minerva can see the bird at the feeder through her mother's crooked left collarbone.

The kettle on the stove whistles.

A door near the bedrooms slams. The cracked teacup lolls on its side, mouth wide and gaping. Minerva's mother wavers and vanishes.

"Min?"

The teacup lies still and just beyond it, the birds flutter around the feeder, frantic and hungry.

"Min, are you all right?"

A hand on her shoulder jolts her from her thoughts. She turns and smiles apologetically at Alex. "Sorry, just thinking."

"Yeah? Concerned about the birds again?" he teases, rubbing one eye and yawning. "They'll be all right."

"The feeder's run low again. I'll have to go to the store."

"They eat that thistle seed like it's their last meal. Want some eggs?"

Minerva nods, glancing back to the place where her mother had twisted and reached. "Think our house is haunted?"

Alex huffs. "I wish. Maybe it'd make this place bearable."

Minerva laughs, despite the uneasy feeling coiling in her gut. They had moved into the small house nearly a year ago and for

Alex, who had always lived in the heart of their bustling city, the neighborhood to the north was uninspiring.

"Over easy?"

"Please."

Alex hurries over to the sink. Minerva feels a chill quiver through her as he walks through the spot where her mother had appeared. She tries to shake off the unease. "I may have to go see my dad."

Alex turns and frowns. "Is something wrong? Did your sister call?"

"Never mind."

"Minerva," he says very carefully, as carefully as he has been lately, ever since their time in couples counseling when Minerva was sure they were ending. "Think about it. You know how your family is. We can sort them out once this marriage chaos is all over. Or you can go now if it's an emergency and I'll fill in the planning gaps while you're gone." But his supposed generosity ruptures with the twitch in the corner of his smile.

She lets out a long sigh even as tension climbs her spine and smiles. "And leave you to order the wrong flowers and get a lemon cake even though I'm allergic to lemon?" Minerva will regret it later; she can already feel the pressure building along the back of her skull. Still…she won't be able to explain it. Not yet. "I'll wait."

"All I do for you, and you have so little faith in me."

"You're burning the eggs."

She is outside, the sun heating her dark hair until it's hot to her touch. Minerva strolls through the yard barefoot, humming along to the woodwind mmuzzz of the cicadas. She turns a corner and Chris looks up from where he kneels in a yellow tulip sea. Minerva stops and knows she is dreaming. Chris is young, his hair still mostly brown, the lines of his face shallower.

"Minerva! I had wondered where you had gotten to! Your ma will be looking for you soon, you know."

Minerva looks down at herself, seeing scraped legs and muddy shorts. She is twelve. She remembers this moment. In twenty minutes, she will find her mother dead in the bathtub.

The waking up is often the worst part. Minerva gasps as she tears out of the dream and the mouthful of air feels like a knife between her ribs. Her coughing wakes Alex and she turns away when he reaches for her.

"Min, are you all right?"

She nods. "Bad dream. I'm sorry."

"Do you want some water?"

"I'll get it."

Minerva escapes down the dark hallway and sneaks into the kitchen, afraid that if she's too loud, her mother will follow.

Minerva's dreams become more lucid the next night and the one following. The fifth night in a row, Alex comes into the dark kitchen where Minerva is sitting cross-legged on the counter with a mug of tea.

"Min, you need sleep."

"I'm okay."

"You're not. You haven't slept more than four hours the past few nights." Alex crosses to her, taking the mug and putting in the sink. He leans on her legs. "Do you want to talk about it?"

"What do you want me to say?"

"We could talk about your dreams. That helps sometimes. Saying what's bothering you out loud."

"Thought you didn't believe in home remedies."

Alex laughs, hooking his arms around her waist and pulling her off the counter. "Come back to bed. I'll show you my favorite home remedy for insomnia."

Minerva slaps his arm, but she's smiling.

Alex holds her close, pressing his cheek against her temple. "What's bothering you?"

"Just thinking about my mom."

Alex kisses her temple, her cheek, her jaw. He holds her in silence for another few moments before he says again: "Come back to bed. We'll do something about it in the morning, all right?"

Minerva is unsure what Alex thinks he can do to combat the haunting, but she lets him guide her back to the bedroom and lies down obediently. Alex pulls the covers up over her and gets into bed a careful distance away, like she's contagious. By the time he's snoring and Minerva can kick off the blankets, she's sweated through her t-shirt. The air presses against her chest and Minerva gasps once before turning her face into her pillow.

She does not sleep and gets up the next morning before Alex. He frowns when he finds her in the kitchen before him. Minerva kisses his cheek and herds him out the door, heading off the conversation she doesn't want to have. She returns to the kitchen to clean up the breakfast dishes.

"You can't tell him." Though, like all times before, she entertains the idea. "Oh, hi, Alex, how was work? By the way, my nightmares—I can see ghosts."

A thistle blossoms at the base of her skull, taking root along her neck, down her spine. She can feel the thistle split open bone and reach in to clutch at her brain. The plate she's holding slips from her grip and clatters into the sink. Minerva takes a deep breath and turns.

Minerva's mother is waiting, gaping eyes ringed with the plum purple of sleepless nights. Self-consciously, Minerva rubs at her own eyes.

Self, insists her mother.

Minerva shakes her head.

Own self.

"Well, you should have appeared sooner. It's *too late*," she snaps, though guilt curls in her stomach. Unfair, the knowledge whispers along the back of her head, disoriented, unusual. Ghosts are like the weather, and though Minerva has seen them before, they have not been hers.

Minerva's mother blinks owlishly and stretches a hand out.

The thistle roots deeper and Minerva yanks open a cabinet, looking for some old wives' antidote. Her fingers snag on a plastic bag and a pound of rice slams onto the counter and spills, grains fanning out in a toothy grin.

Her mother looks more mournful than before and flickers, an old television set, before she is gone.

Minerva presses her fingers against the prickles along the back of her neck as she retrieves a broom and dustpan, weeding out the lingering ache. She sweeps up the rice and her fingers tremble as she picks up the dustpan. *Apparitions can be driven away with rice*, her mother had told her as a child, *that's why they throw rice at weddings.* Once, when she was younger, she had tried to carry a packet of rice with her. Her sister found it in her pocket and scolded her for trying to feed the birds.

Hoisting herself onto the counter, she begins to search the cabinets for aspirin. Minerva fumbles with the bottle and it shudders beneath her grip.

She has not met anyone quite like herself, though Minerva hardly dares to ask. The ghosts are not something someone discusses openly; too personal, too close. The ghosts that drifted about everywhere; old memories that would whisper through her and residues of potent emotions that oozed along the earth seemed only to affect her after a certain age. When she had asked her father why, he had simply grunted, "Ask your mother. This is her idea."

Minerva did not get the chance.

Alex didn't believe what others said about her at first: how she is sickly, prone to bouts of paranoia, nosy, knows things she has no business knowing. They never talked about it when she was around, but their fear and ignorance left sticky tracks that wound about

Minerva's legs. Minerva suspects Alex may believe them now or will soon. She'd done well for a few years now, keeping busy at her job, working in the garden when people's thoughts or emotions or memories got to be too much. A levee against the flood.

Why now, Minerva wonders, why now are things breaking down again.

She sticks her bare feet in the sink and stares out the window over the faucet. Tugging at the charm around her neck, she watches a sparrow preen in the birdbath. When she was younger, Minerva had decided that this must be a gift to *some*one: this perception, this ability to hear the dips in words when someone fibbed, or the ruptures when someone told a blatant lie. Reading the wisps of emotions as if there were fascicles, volumes of a whole.

The extra perception only weighed Minerva down. Perhaps there was some kind of secret to wield it. Some kind of fairy tale genetic lock. She longs for a spindle and a long, long rest.

Minerva swallows the aspirin dry. Can't win them all.

Alex comes home with a bottle of pills. They are not aspirin.

"Try these," he says, handing them to her over dinner.

"What are they?"

"Antigeists. They'll clear up the nightmares."

"This is what you take?"

"It's what everyone takes, Min," Alex answers as he slices into his food too forcefully and the silverware shrieks across the plate. "They do work."

Minerva sets the pill bottle down next to her water glass and thinks, considering the likelihood that the key to her mother's sudden visitations is so easily swallowed. It's been sixteen years since her mother died; there's a reason she has reappeared. Unlike everyone else, Minerva would like to know why she is being haunted, not simply muffle it.

Alex reaches for the bottle, prying it open easily, and shaking a pill out into Minerva's hand. He pushes her water glass forward. "Please, Minerva? Give it a try?"

Marriage, her mother told her once when Minerva had asked why her mother had moved across the country with her father, *is about compromise.*

Minerva swallows the little round pill and tries to take comfort in Alex's smile.

───

Side effects: dizziness, nausea, fatigue, loss of sensitivity, hazy vision, functioning relationships.

───

For three days, Minerva sleeps through the night, waking up only when the late morning sun comes through her blinds. Alex is always gone.

〰

Minerva is grateful for her bicycle commute. Her vision is blurred around the edges like she's in a dream. Her bike seems to know where she's going, for she always ends up at the library, though there are days when she's sure she hasn't been conscious the entire time.

〰

It's like having a head cold. She feels stifled.

Minerva smiles anyway. Marriage is about sacrifice.

〰

A week later, a Saturday, Alex wakes up late and finds Minerva in the tiny garden tucked into their small yard.

"Better, then?" he asks, standing a safe distance away as if she'll lob a trowel at him for disrupting her piles of dirt.

Minerva brushes the dirt off of her knees as she stands and peels off her dirty gardening gloves. She considers the honest answer that while her mother has not reappeared, she feels like she's looking in a mirror after a hot shower. Minerva glances up at Alex, standing uncertainly at the edge of her retreat. Compromise. "Yes, thank you."

"What're you planting there? Won't it freeze?"

"It shouldn't," Minerva tells him. "Not in March."

Alex looks up at the sky, squinting. "I don't know—don't those look like snow clouds brewing up there?"

"Stop. Don't you know that part of gardening is being optimistic about the weather?" She hands him her trowel and a small seed envelope. "Start planting. Happy thoughts."

Alex digs up an etched silver ring that is nearly identical to the one Minerva's mother had been buried with. He passes it to Minerva and leaves soon after, another day hard at work.

Minerva wipes the dirt off of the ring and steeps it in some jewelry cleaner. She rubs the back of her neck. Something lingers there, waiting for her to turn around.

It's just the wedding stress, pumpkin, her father will say if she calls him up. Lie down for a bit. Take some time off from planning and work. Things will work out.

Minerva presses a cool palm against her forehead, trying to absorb the silent morning calm of the sun-soaked kitchen. If she starts becoming restless again, Alex will ask questions, things she can't answer. The ghosts weren't too unusual and could be "solved" with medication. Communicating with them was very different.

Alex will figure out that the medication will only work for so long, she supposes, and her skin prickles at the thought of the more extreme solutions, surgeries and invasive therapy. It's treatable when detected early, but Minerva has seen ghosts since she was a child.

She is past help. She is an extreme case, something they'll want to study. Pick at her until she's down to her cold bones.

It rains for the next week. Alex asks Minerva to stay inside and call in sick to work, as if she is prone to catching her death from a little damp, but Minerva cannot stay in a house where the ghosts are not visible.

11

"Lovely weather we're having," a voice says above the wind whistling through the library's leaky windows.

Minerva looks up from her place behind the reference desk. "If you're a fan of spring, I guess so." She feels tired and her body aches. It feels like she's fighting an infection.

"I'm not," the young woman answers with a grin.

Minerva considers her. She is just a few years younger than Minerva, she estimates, definitely shorter. Cropped, dye-dark hair, nose ring, and a tangle of inked lines spilling out from the neck of her t-shirt. There is a brightness about her and Minerva feels something ease in her usually cool exterior.

"I'm Minerva," she offers her hand.

The woman takes it. "Anaïs."

Anaïs's ring bites into her palm, the crease that Minerva's mother always called her *lifeline*, and a memory that is not her own bursts into her body.

She selects a few plastic capsules before taking a seat before a young man, thin with a round face. She pulls open a sealed package and loads the tattoo gun, whistling.

"Muzetta's Waltz," says the young man—the customer. The tattoo parlor around them is quiet, only a murmur from the bustling city winding through the cracks in the windows and the door.

She beams. "Yeah, good ear." She snaps a needle into the gun. "Are you a music major?"

He shrugs, a fluid roll through his shoulders.

"Undecided?"

23

"I have time."

She laughs and tries not to think about the scar she's tattooing over. She wipes down the underside of his forearm. "Ready? It's going to sting."

He smiles at her, a lazy expression which brags, I've had worse.

She hums around the buzz of the needle; the young man hardly moves and never complains. As she wipes excess ink from his wrist, she notices his gaze following the line of one of her more narrative tattoos, exposed today by the hot weather and broken air conditioning.

"It's like a badge," she tells him. "A purple heart; you and I choose to possess, rather than be possessed." She doesn't mention how terrified she had been when she finally let a tattoo artist put ink to her barely-healed skin. The first of many, joyous and tragic, until her skin was a roadmap, an intimacy if she allowed someone to read the full narrative.

"Make sure to keep it clean and moisturized," she continues. "The surface'll heal in about two weeks, but it'll take longer for it to heal completely. Try not to expose it to too much sun."

The young man pays, leaves a generous tip, and slouches out the door. He weaves smoothly through the drunk crowds and vanishes. She stares after him, thinking of the tattoo he had requested—the petit prince, *suspended between life and death, poised to fall with his hands clasped over his face and a lone, lopsided star quietly vigilant in the distance—and hums Muzetta's Waltz to herself as the vibrations of the el tracks roll up her legs.*

Her palm is slippery against the desk when Minerva pulls back. Her hands tingle and head throbs from the information she just absorbed. Minerva blinks and distantly notes that Anaïs looks startled.

"Are you all right?"

Minerva nods, wiping her palms on her pant legs, swallowing against the nausea pressing up her throat. "Yes, fine. Dizzy spell."

Anaïs glances at her curiously but steps back. "Nice to meet you, Minerva," she says. "I don't suppose you could direct me to the graphic novels?"

Minerva raises a shaky hand and points. Anaïs smiles. The woven knot of dark lines curling along her shoulder form a shape. A skull grins at Minerva, a brand glowing through the cotton fabric. Its mouth unhinges and gapes at Minerva, accusation burning in its empty sockets.

"Ashes to ashes. Dust to dust."

When Minerva gets home that night, she collapses into bed and doesn't dream. She rises the next morning still exhausted, still alone in the bed. Alex greets her when Minerva walks into the kitchen and hands her a cup of tea and a pill. Her stomach rolls at the sight of it, but she takes it.

Alex kisses her and heads out the door.

Minerva excuses herself during her evening shift at the library and vomits in the bathroom. She is pale, she sees in the mirror, and her skin is burning. Something inside of her screams, though she doesn't know what. Her hand clenches around her coffee mug and something tears away at her.

"Go home," her supervisor says. "You look like death."

The clothes are winding and twisting in the faint evening light when Minerva arrives home. She flips on every light as she walks through the house, stopping in the kitchen to read a note taped next to the phone.

A t-shirt smacks the window and Minerva jumps. She opens the side door. The cool air is refreshing against her still-feverish skin. She slips outside. The breeze is picking up. Minerva ducks through the waving clothes, testing the clothespins, and secures the shirt.

Her forearm prickles. Minerva turns and her mother reaches from between a pair of old jeans and her favorite sweater.

Self. Own self, she says.

Minerva stumbles backward, her arms tangling in towels as she lands hard on her wrist. Her mother reaches again.

Be. True.

"Go away!"

The wind howls, swallowing their voices and twisting, mixing words until Minerva hears clearly: *To thine own self, be true.* Then her mother's ghost fades, swept away in the windstorm.

Hamlet—Minerva blinks. How perfectly like her mother.

Minvera's hand is bleeding onto the slick lawn; a thistle curls low in the grass. She turns and her dinner comes up. Minerva crawls away from where she's been sick and lies back, staring up at the sky. The night smells like yellow streetlights and emptiness.

Minerva is there for hours, her skin heating the ground, her body shivering. Her mother walks out of the kitchen when Minerva stumbles back inside. Alex is not there.

The ring she found in the garden is there. She fishes it out of the bowl and dries it. Minerva tries it on. The ring slips easily onto her finger and stays, like it belongs.

In the morning, she leaves the house and wanders into a coffee shop. The barista is familiar.

"Anaïs," Minerva says.

Anaïs blinks then smiles. "Minerva, yeah? No library today?"

"I'm taking a break."

"Away from all those dusty books?"

"I don't mind the dusty books."

"So, just need some time away?"

Minerva smiles. Anaïs laughs, embarrassed.

When Anaïs turns to make Minerva's coffee, Minerva notices a young girl sitting in the far corner of the coffee shop. The girl's hair is long and painfully straight; her face is clean and without makeup. She's reading a comic book.

She is still wearing the ring when Alex returns that evening. Dinner is made and served in silence, Alex staring at Minerva as she moves around the kitchen. She still feels the slow, congested movements, but things are loosening. The ghosts are visible again, and the tension has spilled down her neck.

Alex knows something is different. Minerva can see it in the lines of his mouth as he puzzles over her. "Why weren't you at work the other day?"

"My supervisor sent me home," Minerva replies. "I was throwing up."

"And now?"

"I'm fine."

"How have the, um. The pills?"

Minerva notices he lowers his voice, as if the neighbors may overhear that she takes some sort of medication and judge them.

"You sure you're all right?"

Minerva shies away from Alex's hand and rounds the counter. "I'm fine. I'm just…"

"Stressed? We can still hire a wedding planner, if that's what this is about."

"We can't afford that, Alex."

Alex opens his mouth to reply, but a high-pitched ring cuts him off. He rummages around his papers and open briefcase before he finds his cell phone. Alex silences it and turns back to Minerva.

"We can ask your father for a bit more money. You know he doesn't mind."

"No."

"But Minerva—"

"*No.* I don't want to ask him for that. It's not important."

Alex's expression is pinched like he wants to argue, but he holds up his hands in concession instead. Turning, he sweeps all of his stuff into his briefcase, snapping it shut.

"Where are you going?"

"I forgot something."

Minerva watches Alex leave, storming through the doorway and through the apparition of her mother who has been watching the whole fight.

"How'd you end up working here?" Minerva asks, watching Anaïs clean out the espresso machine. "You don't look the type."

"Oh? What type do I look like, then?"

Tattoo artist. "Graphic designer."

"It's the tattoos, isn't it?"

"It's the kind of tattoos. Non-traditional. Like watercolors."

"You know more about tattoos than I would have expected." Anaïs turns to give her a once-over. "You got a half-sleeve under that cardigan or something?"

"I'm full of surprises," Minerva quips lightly, watching her perception of Anaïs sharpen. The tattoos flicker on her skin, like an old bulb.

———

Alex calls and Minerva leaves, forgetting her drink.

———

Anaïs appears at the reference desk when Minerva is working the next morning. Without preamble, she places a steaming cup in front of Minerva. "There's the drink I owe you."

"Oh. Well, you didn't have to."

"I did, actually," Anaïs replies, embarrassed. "What kind of barista am I to forget an order? The owner would kill me if she found out how I was treating her customers."

Minerva takes a sip. "It's not entirely your fault. You can blame me if you like. I did run out."

"I'm not going to tell her, period. She'll have half my pay for 'damages.'"

"Yes, I'm terribly damaged." Minerva hides her answering smile in her drink. She doesn't see Anaïs slip a heavy book into the book drop. "Thanks. I could use a hot drink today."

"Yeah, well, anytime you need one, come on in. On the house." She starts for the door.

"Does that include your other job, too?" Minerva calls, ignoring the severe looks from patrons.

Anaïs's posture twitches and she flashes a grin over her shoulder.

Minerva watches Anaïs stroll through the automatic doors and into the parking lot before she swivels and scoops up a few books lingering in the bottom of the book drop return bin. The residue, left with borrower's fingerprints, curls around Minerva's fingers like damp fog.

With a nod to the other woman working at the desk with her, Minerva weaves between the shelves until she finds the series of numbers that match the books in her arms. The first slides easily back into place, but the second requires more effort. The last, heavy with glossy comic pages, shifts against Minerva's bare forearm, and her knees give out. The reverberations of the dropped book are distant, like an echo, before her awareness—which had never had a sense of timing—swallows her.

"Are you cheating?"

"What kind of question is that?"

"Just answer it. Please."

"Minerva, how can you ask me something like that—do you know what I do for us? For this wedding? I'm slaving away at a job that I hate *so you can have some wedding you've been dreaming about since you were twelve."*

"Where did you—I have not been dreaming about this wedding since I was twelve! What on earth made you think that?"

"All girls dream of their wedding. My own sister had a scrapbook."

"I do not have a scrapbook, Alex."

"Well, whatever. This is the wedding you want and I—we're—making sacrifices for it. We could be living in the city-city, *you know, not this stupid 'neighborhood.' We could have a nice apartment and a small ceremony, but instead we're out here in a house we can only afford because I'm putting in overtime and you're working. You're not even supposed to be working, Minerva. You know what your health is like!...How could you even think that I'm cheating on you?"*

"What does all that have to do with my question? If you're working so hard, Alex, why do you come home smelling like perfume and smoke?"

"The guys and I go out for some drinks afterwards. And yeah, sometimes there are some women flirting, but there's no harm in just talking to them. We don't talk much anymore, you know!"

Then Minerva feels it, the other meaning, the one Alex wants to say but has pulled back at the last minute: If you weren't so distant. If you weren't so cold.

"It's always the same perfume."

"What?"

"Alex, it's always the same."

Alex is still, the lines of his body rigid, and Minerva's accusation lingers like wisps of tobacco smoke. Minerva waits for the bite she knows is lurking in the dark corners of their words, lying in wait. Alex lunges—he kicks over a chair—Minerva's grandmother's antique vase crumples on the tile floor.

Minerva's hair is sticking to the back of her neck as the voices fade into the silence of the library. There's a cool hand patting her cheek and as the other voices waver in and out like a poorly-tuned radio, another takes their place.

"Minerva. Minerva, can you hear me?"

"I…" she blinks. "Anaïs?"

Anaïs smiles, but it's shaky at best. "Back in the world of the living, then?"

There's a bitter taste in her mouth and she's weak. Minerva has never had a vision like that before. She has never had one that *predicted*. "What happened?"

"You fainted," Anaïs answers, her mouth folding into a frown as Minerva gets to her feet, leaning heavily against the bookshelves. "And you look like you're about to faint again."

Minerva shakes her head, dismissing the idea as she kicks off her heels and stands in her stocking feet. "I never faint twice."

"Really?" The affected surprise is strained, a lie tightly woven in only one word. Anaïs looks down, fingers twisted self-consciously into her hair.

As her heartbeat slows to a normal pace, and her stomach settles, something else occurs to her. "How did you find me down here?"

Anaïs looks at her feet and then nervously adjusts the line of books on the shelves at her right. Her fingers linger on the graphic novel, a familiar touch along the spine. "I…uh, well, just luck. I realized I had forgotten to get a book I wanted and well…"

The words sound steady enough, but Minerva can hear the quiver lurking under "just luck." She mulls over this for a moment, watching Anaïs fiddle with the books and then one of the earrings she's wearing. Minerva opens her mouth to say something. Before she can speak, a chilly sigh rolls through the library.

"Drafty in here."

"Not usually," Minerva replies, already scanning the gaps between book and shelf for their approaching guest. She's expecting her mother to reappear with another unhelpful clue. Instead, the girl from the coffee shop turns the corner and waits at the end of the row.

"Can I help you?" Minerva calls.

Behind Minerva, Anaïs makes a choked noise.

"You can see her?" Minerva asks Anaïs, her eyes on the girl.

"Everyone can see her," Anaïs answers and her voice is shaking. "Most people just ignore her."

"Who is she?" Minerva asks, watching the girl pull on her hair. "She looks…" *familiar*, she wants to say, but Anaïs, with an odd look on her face, picks up her dropped bag.

"I have to go," she says. "Bye, Minerva."

As Anaïs turns the corner at the end of the row of shelves, so, too, does the girl. Minerva returns all the scattered books to their places, not daring to touch the graphic novel again. She folds her prickling arms and goes back upstairs to clock out for the afternoon, uneasy with the memory of what's to come.

⁓

Alex is ecstatic when he returns home on time for dinner and finds Thai food from his favorite restaurant on the table. "What's the catch?" he asks, after eating his fill.

"Nothing," Minerva says, watching the perfume on his clothing curl into a smoky form over his shoulder. "No catch."

He smiles at her like he used to, when they first met. Something hollows out inside of Minerva.

When Alex dozes on the couch later, the news projecting along his rumpled work clothes, Minerva walks quietly across the room. She puts her grandmother's vase away in a cabinet and flushes the rest of the antigeists.

<hr />

"Do you want to get lunch some time?"

Anaïs gives Minerva a funny half-smile. "Sure. How do you feel about going to that noodle house around the corner?"

"Minerva? Minerva!"

"In the living room!"

Alex walks through the doorway into the peaceful room where Minerva has been sitting since she returned home from work.

"What are you doing?"

"Just thinking," Minerva answers.

"About what?"

She shrugs. "Nothing."

"Have you just been sitting here all afternoon?"

"I was reading earlier. Did a little work around the house before that. Gardening, things like that."

"You didn't make dinner."

Minerva glances over at him, squinting through the late afternoon sunlight. "No."

"Why not?"

"For goodness's sake, Alex," Minerva says sharply, "do I have to do everything for you?"

He stares at her; Minerva wonders how long she's been swallowing complaints.

"Fine," Alex says. "I'll see you later."

The door slams and rattles the plate window in the door.

Alex comes back just after four a.m. and falls into the bed beside her. He smells of something ashy and thick, like rot and cremation, smoke and something sweet, nearly hidden.

Minerva presses her face into her pillow and Alex starts to snore.

⸻

Things are quiet again. Minerva cooks, gardens and works until she's too exhausted at night to dream, and it works for a while. Her mother watches her, mostly while she gardens. The thistles are choking out the carrots she and Alex planted last month.

Alex comes home late and is gone early. She sleeps through his presence at her side.

⸻

Anaïs kisses Minerva after the third time they meet for a meal. Her fingers are light along the back of Minerva's neck and Minerva can smell the shampoo in her hair—lemongrass and lavender: a sharp, clean smell.

⸻

They fight. Minerva's grandmother's vase remains whole, hidden in a cabinet far from their dispute.

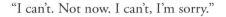

"I can't. Not now. I can't, I'm sorry."

"Why are there so many thistles cropping up?" Alex asks, standing at the kitchen window. "Did all the birdseed sprout or something?"

Minerva stands behind him, barefoot, wearing the shorts and t-shirt she slept in, chipped tea mug in hand. "I'll dig them up this afternoon."

Alex turns to look at her. He's in one of his favorite suits, collar ironed, tie knotted perfectly. The contrast of her worn-in clothes and his neat appearance is not lost on her.

"You're sure you're fine? Your medication is working okay?"

"Yes."

"You could just get some weed killer. I'll leave you some money for it."

"It'll kill all the grass," Minerva counters. "I'll dig them up." She looks over his shoulder to the world outside.

Alex crosses the kitchen and puts his hands on her shoulders. "Min, I don't want you to strain yourself."

Minerva watches her mother peek in the sliding door. Minerva's gaze slides back to Alex's. She thinks of the smoke that has been clinging to him, choking her away from him, and of Anaïs, whom

41

she hasn't seen in a week, but is patiently awaiting an invitation to something more than just lunch. "When you're ready," she had said.

Minerva puts the mug down and grabs Alex by the front of his pressed shirt, kissing him. Alex jerks in surprise at the cloudburst of energy when she has been lethargic for months now. He kisses her back, but pulls away to say, "I have to go to work."

Minerva doesn't listen and presses her body against his, into his, like smoke seeping into his clothing. Alex gives in, holding her against him, kissing her like he did when they were newly in love, sneaking moments together between classes.

But the memory wavers and fades and Alex pulls away. "Min, I'm sorry—I have a big meeting, first thing."

Minerva nods once. "I love you," she calls after him, casting a line for his response.

"I love you, too."

The words shake and fall apart.

≈

Minerva gets dressed and goes to work. It's a slow morning, a Wednesday. Someone returns a graphic novel.

"Lisa," she says to the other woman seated at the desk with her, breaking the silence she's kept since arriving at work, "I'm going to go get some coffee. Do you want anything?"

"I know hardly anything about you. What's your family like?"

Minerva taps her finger against the side of her glass. "Traditional."

"Ah."

"Yours?"

She grins. "I'm a tattooed barista with an arts degree and who is saving up to open her own tattoo parlor. What does that tell you?"

"That your family is either highly eccentric or conservative."

"Fair."

"My dad's rich."

"And you decided to be a librarian?"

"I didn't say I was traditional."

"Well, you're a regular rebel. No white picket fence for you."

Smoke drifts across the room and Minerva's pasta sticks in her throat. Anaïs passes her a water glass.

"You're worried."

"No," Minerva insists. "No, I'm not."

"Oh—um, right. Sorry. I meant to say you looked worried. Looked."

"It's nothing. Just thinking."

"About what?"

"Nothing."

"OK."

Minerva lets Anaïs bring her up to her apartment. A roadmap of intimacy, but Minerva only reads half the narrative before she remembers herself and spills her secrets.

I think you should go.

IV

The day is bright, sunny, and warm. Minerva calls in sick to work and sits against the shed with her morning tea tucked between her knees. Alex's shadow falls across her legs and she looks up to find him staring critically at the slippers she's worn through the grass and the drawstring shorts hiked up and showing the birthmark high on her thigh.

"I thought you were going to work," she says, sipping her now-lukewarm tea.

"I can go in later," Alex answers. Then, "are you having one of your...?"

"One of my what?"

"You know. Funny moments. Swoons."

Minerva sighs and looks across the unkempt lawn. "I'm not some character from a Victorian novel."

Alex shuffles down to sit next to her. "You sure?"

"Did you call in to work because you thought I was unwell?"

"Well...you've been acting strange lately. I was worried."

Strange because she spent an afternoon relaxing and doing things she liked, rather than what should have been done. Minerva bristles at the implication, that Alex doesn't pay enough attention to see she's been spending time with someone else. "I'm fine," Minerva says again, thinking of her vase and Anaïs's strained expression.

"Yeah," Alex says, unconvinced. "D'you know you walked out here in your slippers?"

"They have rubber bottoms."

"And in your pajamas?"

Minerva looks at him. "The yard is fenced. No one will see."

"Good thing," Alex murmurs to himself, glancing down at the freckles on Minerva's pale legs. "Minerva, are you sure you're all right? You haven't been yourself since your mother…"

"My mother what?" Minerva asks her tea. She spots a thistle two feet from her right foot, makes a note to dig it up once Alex goes to work.

"You know," he says under his breath. "Since she. Showed up."

Minerva looks up, startled.

"I know, we're not supposed to talk about it, but Minerva, she's *here*."

"Has she spoken to you?"

"Spoken—no, of course not. You know they don't talk."

"Of course," Minerva hears herself say.

"I think you should go to the doctor. We can afford a check-up and my job'll cover the prescription costs. No more of the over-the-counter antigeists. We'll get the strong stuff."

"You want me to take stronger medication? Shut it all out?" Minerva asks, looking at Alex. The early morning sunlight spills across his face, butterfly kisses along his neck and shoulders, and Minerva remembers the first morning she woke up next to him.

"No. No. Want is the wrong word. I think you should—what I *want* is us to be like we were. Before." Alex runs a hand over his face. "Look, I'm going to take them, too. I mean, I can see…I've got the same problem. Maybe it'll be a bonding experience," he tries with a smile that tells Minerva, you freak you did this to me you you you.

I've got the same problem, he said. Singular. Minerva's mother.

48

Minerva hands Alex her empty mug and gets to her feet, walking across the yard and back into the house. She tucks herself into the dry tub and listens to Alex crash through the house. By the time she reemerges, Alex has gone into work. Her mug lies beached in the dry sink.

Minerva gets a shovel from the garage and digs up every thistle in the yard, still wearing her slippers.

"Good morning, how can—oh. Hello."

"Hi," Minerva says back. "I missed the morning rush?"

"Just a bit, yeah. What can I get for you?"

"Do you have anything that'll restore peace of mind?"

Anaïs's mouth tightens. "Do you need me to call someone?"

"No! No, I don't want to go back to that house. She's waiting for me."

"Okay." Anaïs eyes Minerva's legs, crisscrossed with red scratches, mud, and grass stains. "Minerva, do you know you wore your slippers here?"

"They have rubber bottoms."

"Ah. Of course." Anaïs pauses. "How about a shower?"

Minerva turns her head to look at Anaïs. "A shower?"

"Yeah. I mean, don't take this the wrong way, but you look like you could use it."

Minerva gives a shaky smile at that.

Anaïs flips the *open* sign to *closed* and locks the front door. "Come on. Let's get you cleaned up."

Minerva laughs hoarsely and lets Anaïs pull her along. She leads Minerva to a winding back corridor and unlocks an impressive amount of locks on a door hidden in an alcove.

"Side entrance," Anaïs explains. "Top of the stairs. The blue door. If you don't remember."

Minerva remembers: Anaïs's apartment is a snug, but cheery place. Sunlight tumbles through the tall bay windows and spills across the wood floors. It's quiet even when there are people in it.

Anaïs disappears down the hallway for a minute and returns with a towel and a stack of clothing. "The bathroom is the open door down there."

"Thanks."

"Yep," Anaïs says, turning away to rummage through her cabinets.

Minerva turns the shower on hot and stands under the water for a minute or two before she finds the lavender shampoo she's smelled on Anaïs before and scrubs it into her hair until her scalp feels raw. She towels herself off, dresses in the jeans and long-sleeved shirt Anaïs has given her, and winds her wet hair back into a bun. The tea is on the table when she emerges; Anaïs is peeling an orange over the trashcan.

"How do you do it?"

Anaïs looks up. "Do what? Peel an orange?"

Minerva shakes her head and waves a hand. "No. You know… predict."

Anaïs flushes. "I don't know what you're talking about."

"You do. You shouldn't be scared of it."

"Who says I'm scared?"

"You warned me about a fight with my fiancé. So I hid the vase he was set to break and tried to head off the argument." Minerva tilts her head. "Didn't you ever try that?"

"Yeah. Lots of times."

"Why are you afraid?"

Anaïs laughs in disbelief. "Oh, I don't know. Maybe because I'll wake up one day, see my own death, and not be able to do anything about it?"

"The future is relative. It must be."

"Your tea's getting cold. There's honey in the cabinet if you want some."

"It has to be," Minerva insists. "Why else would you have this gift?"

"The gods hate me?" Anaïs guesses.

Hours later, Minerva interrupts the radio murmuring on the counter as Anaïs puts together a snack. "I never thanked you for that warning."

"What warning?"

"About the vase. I think—I *know* things would have gotten much worse if Alex had broken it during our fight."

"Actually. When did I warn you?" Anaïs asks after standing in silence. "I don't remember saying anything to you. I wouldn't have. We hardly know each other."

"I…I just knew."

"No one 'just knows.' Come on, I dumped all my skeletons out—well, most of them—now it's your turn."

Minerva shrugs, an uncomfortable wiggle in the corner where she's been pinned. "I've never been much of a talker."

"Ah, well." Anaïs looks at her feet, hands on her hips. "Lucky me, then?"

"Depends on how you look at it," Minerva tells her.

"You must ooze trustworthiness. I suppose that's a better reason to trust you than 'I'm bonkers.'"

"I'm sorry. I didn't mean." Minerva swallows. "There's no excuse."

"No," Anaïs agrees, looking at her steadily, "There's not."

"I can explain."

"I'm sure you can."

"Do you think it's weird, having skeletons to clean out of your closet when you're only in your late twenties?"

Anaïs blinks, her face blank. "Is this a trick question?"

"No."

"Then no. Why the spring cleaning?"

"The shelves need dusting."

"Brave," Anaïs says after a pause. "Most people I know just get tattoos."

"What good does that do?"

Anaïs shrugs. "It's like a badge or a medal. Something that allows you to take control of what's happened to you, rather than let the event control you. It's…it can be soothing."

The sentiment is familiar, the echo itching along Minerva's forearm. "Did it work for you?"

Anaïs laughs, startled. "I suppose it did, yes."

"Can I ask you a personal question?"

"I think you just did."

"Who is she?"

"Who?"

Minerva points to the corner of the kitchen where the young girl sits, staring out the window.

Anaïs looks shaken. "No one. An old memory. It doesn't matter. Nobody ever takes notice of her."

"You do."

"It was a long time ago; I'm not who I used to be." She blurts, like it's an excuse. The silence that follows is thick, palpable. Butter on toast.

"I'm sorry. I didn't mean to pry."

"Yes, you did. You like to pry."

"It's hard not to."

"I guess so. Your own tattoos."

Minerva gives a small smile at the comparison. "My tattoos," she agrees. Possessing, rather than be possessed, but it's beginning to fray around the edges of identity.

"Thanks for the apology even if it wasn't all that genuine."

"It was. I meant to pry, but I didn't mean to hurt." Minerva shrugs. "I suppose that's something else I've never been very good at."

"Can I ask…? We all have our ghosts that follow us and some of us can shut them out. The lucky ones."

"They're not lucky."

"No?"

"Burying yourself so deeply to try and forget something that once hurt you?" Minerva shakes her head. "It's hardly lucky to be able to forget yourself. What you've been through. You can't go through life without only half of what's made you who you are."

"Gets crowded in the dusty closets? And under the rugs?"

"Something like that."

"So." Anaïs takes a shaky breath. "Who follows you?"

"Everyone."

"So who do you shut out and who do you keep?"

≡≡≡

Minerva is waiting when her mother reappears.

"What do you want?" Minerva asks.

Her mother says nothing. She looks as Minerva remembers her: dressed well, but subdued and distant. Unhappy.

"Compromise," she says, finally. "Not sacrifice."

54

"I have to go see my family. I won't be long."

Alex sits back. "Look, Min," he says on an exhaled breath. "I'm trying to be patient, I really am. But this—it's too much."

Minerva puts the last of the dirty dishes in the sink and rests her wrists on the edge of the counter. It would figure that once she knew how to relieve one pressure in her life another would slide into place, her mother's ghost trading places with her fiancé's temper.

"I won't be long," Minerva reminds him, "just a few days, maybe as long as a week."

His chair shrieks on the tile when Alex pushes back from the table. He paces with angry, shuffling steps. "I'm doing this for you, you know."

Minerva takes a deep breath, waiting and watching as Alex clears the table.

"Well?"

"Well what, Alex?"

"You're not saying anything."

"I don't know what you want me to say," Minerva answers, feeling the honesty loosen the tension coiled in her ribcage. "I'm not sure there's anything I *can* say."

"How about an acknowledgment, at least? A sentence that makes me think *something* is going on—that you *see*."

"That I see?" Minerva starts. "I *see* that you're working hard, Alex, but the perfume I *smell* on your clothes nightly is another thing."

"Come on, that was from the bar—I can't help it if someone *flirts*—"

"Every night for a week, Alex?"

"Nothing happened, I was just talking!" he starts forward then thinks better of it. "And what about you? I've been putting up with a lot lately, Minerva, and I can hardly take it. I've tried to be patient, but I can't stand it anymore, your mother just hanging around. And you're off in some other world, like you can't hear me or I don't matter or whatever. How am I supposed to get married to someone like that? Someone who's so caught up in things in the past that I have to scream to be heard?"

"If you would just listen," Minerva cuts in and she feels Alex's surprise tingle through her fingertips at the steel in her voice. "I'm trying to fix this. Something's wrong and I have to go sort it out. This is the only way."

"The only way is for you to drop an insane amount of money on a last minute plane ticket when we're barely keeping ourselves out of debt as it is?"

"Alex, please."

"You don't even know what she wants."

"Yes I do." The answer sticks in her throat and the dish shivers in her hands.

"Min, how could you? They don't talk. They never talk; they just hang around. Look, if she's giving you that much trouble, we can—"

The dish cracks.

"Minerva?"

"I can hear them."

"What?"

"Alex, I can hear them." She rubs a soapy hand across her forehead. "And other things too. Old memories. Emotions. It's like drowning."

Alex crosses the room. He cups her cheek though anger still shakes his palms. "Are you feeling well? You haven't got a fever."

"I feel *fine*. I can't just shut it off like the rest of the world with a few convenient pills."

"You were starting to sleep better; I thought maybe those pills were working." His expression slowly softens as worry sets in.

"Alex, you're not listening."

"Minerva, you're not listening to *yourself*. Listening to ghosts? You'd have to be some kind of—of—"

"She's restless."

Alex stops and considers her for a long moment. His sigh is resigned. "Off you go, then. I never did expect you to stay in one place."

"No, that's not what—"

"*Minerva*," Alex interrupts. "Take a week off. Go and see your father. I could use a break from your mother hanging around, you know."

VI

The flight is unremarkable and the cab ride to her parents' house only notable because of the car her father sends to meet her. Dread shivers up Minerva's spine as they pull up the long driveway and old worries stir. Minerva takes a few breaths, wondering how she had ever managed to forget the stuffiness characteristic to her childhood home.

The house is just as she remembers it: a cozy two-story home set back behind rows of tall pine trees. The forest covers the rest of their property, save for a small backyard cut out of the wilderness, just enough to fit a generous garden and a swing set. She has just taken her bag out of the trunk when her father appears, coming down the steps.

Each time Minerva sees her father in person, she is reminded of how little she resembles him. Her father is a tanned, broad-shouldered man, loud and often intimidating to the neighborhood kids who cut their lawn for a small fee. Minerva is thin and pale with what her mother used to refer to as "bird bones."

"How's my youngest, then?" he booms, opening his arms for a hug. "How's that entrepreneur fiancé of yours?"

"He's fine. A little stressed out with his newest project."

"Well, that's to be expected. Do you need help with your suitcase?"

"I just have the carry-on." Minerva catches the doubtful look on her father's face. "I'm only staying a few days."

"You can stay as long as you like, you know. I haven't changed any of the bedrooms around at all. I had them cleaned, don't look at me like that. Just had fresh sheets put on your bed this afternoon."

"Thank you."

"Sweetheart, if you're having doubts about the wedding—"

Minerva stops and tries to hide her shock by unbuttoning her light jacket and hanging it up in the closet herself. "Who said I have doubts about the wedding?"

Her father shrugs. "Something Vienna mentioned."

Minerva sighs. "How is Vienna?"

"Keeping busy balancing her job and family. You know your sister."

Not busy enough to keep from prying into my life as usual, Minerva thinks but doesn't say it.

"Minnie, if you have doubts, you ought to take more time to plan. Don't rush into things you're unsure of."

"I have been meaning to ask, where did you scatter mother's ashes?"

"Don't be so absurd, Minerva," her father scolds. "What kind of question is that when you're barely two minutes in the door and haven't even asked about your other sisters? Why don't you go rest in your old room until dinner."

"But—"

"We're eating at seven." With that, Minerva's father strides out of the room and in the direction of his study.

Minerva turns and obediently goes up to her room, her feet aching. She sits down on her bed and toes off the heels she wore during the trip. The old memories of the house settle onto her chest and the tension she had previously escaped winds through her body.

On windy nights, ghosts from the old forest sweep through the screened windows. Minerva crosses to her window and shuts it before she drifts off into a light doze, waking when the smell of dinner wafts into her room.

"Can't imagine what it could be," Chris, the gardener and one of her grandfather's friends, is saying when Minerva takes her place at the table. "Good evening, Minerva, you are looking well."

"Hello, Chris, how are you?"

"Oh, just fine. Garden's another matter."

Minerva glances at her father and he fills in, "Chris was just telling me there's been an unusual problem with weeds lately."

"I've never seen something like this before," Chris confirms, scratching at the graying stubble along his jaw. "We've never had such a problem with weeds—almost like it's an invasive species that hasn't been documented yet."

"I highly doubt thistles can be classified as an 'invasive species.'"

Minerva glances up. "Thistles? Those have been turning up in our yard, too."

Chris frowns, looking down at the silverware on the table. The dim lighting catches the wrinkles on his face, a tiny, tortuous irrigation system constructed from a lifetime out in the bright summer sun. "We've been pulling 'em out as soon as they sprout, but they're growing like…well, growing like weeds, I suppose."

"I thought we always had them in the yard." Minerva specifically remembers stepping on several barefoot over the course of many summers when shoes were not conducive to her habitual exploring.

"Not like this. This is just unreasonable."

"When did it start?"

"Oh, a few months back, I'd say. I'm afraid they choked out all those beautiful daffodils you had us plant for Tess not long after she passed, Malcolm." Chris sighs. "I couldn't even salvage the bulbs."

"Deer might still like them," her father says, taking a long drink from his glass of beer.

Minerva wants to ask more questions, but dinner is served before she can open her mouth. She eats quietly, unsettled.

"Dad?"

"In the study, Minnie!"

Minerva crosses into the room. When she was growing up, it was her father's private sanctuary away from the world of a three-woman household. Minerva hesitates before she enters, old memories in her feet, though the room, like most of the house, seems to have stayed a constant during the passage of time.

"What are you doing?"

"Just some work, odds and ends. Nothing interesting."

Minerva nods, eyes straying to the small, framed photo of her parents, years younger, turned away from her father. She reaches to turn it around.

"Was there something you wanted?"

Minerva yanks her hand back. "Um, yes."

"Oh, don't say 'um,' Minerva. No one will take you seriously."

Her young mother looks up at Minerva from the frame with a familiar expression. Self-doubting or hesitant. Unhappy, for certain.

"Well, Minerva?"

"You didn't answer my question before."

"What question was that?"

"Mom's remains."

"You were there at the service," her father mutters, looking down at the papers stacked in front of him. "Don't you remember?"

"It was a while ago. I thought she wanted to be cremated and have her ashes scattered."

"Well, your mother was a free spirit, that's for certain. Didn't much like doing things ways that one should."

"So you never scattered her ashes?"

"They're interred in the family tomb. Tradition."

Minerva goes back upstairs. Her headache has returned.

⁓

The next few days are full of stiff politeness and laden with pockets of unspoken secrets. The house is cold, unhappy, and filled with more spite than Minerva remembers, and the warm beams filled with happy memories have all but vanished. She sleeps restlessly under the press of nightmares and ghosts that can't quite form.

"Your sister is on the phone."

"What does she want?"

"She heard about your visit."

Minerva takes the phone from her father and braces herself for the comments she knows are coming.

"Hi, Vienna."

"Min, how are you doing?"

"I'm fine."

"Dad says your relationship with Alex has hit a rough patch."

Minerva considers telling her sister—her goody-too-shoes, has-never-fucked-up sister—about what she's done. Lied. Cheated. Thrown away her prescriptions because they were doing their job too well. Is the cheating less bad if I was cheated on first? Minerva wonders, standing in barefoot silence.

"Yes. We're trying time apart."

"Well, marriage and relationships are tough. Sometimes, you need to be apart. Compatibility isn't 24/7."

"I know."

"Oh, Minerva, I know you know. I'm just saying. I'm your big sister after all."

"How are Dan and the kids?"

"Oh, fine. They're out for the day, doing some kind of activity that involves a lot of mud and sweating. Hiking, probably."

"Oh."

"Listen, I know you're avoiding the topic, but I'm going to tell you anyway. Take the time you need, but check in with Alex while you're back. He deserves to know how you're doing, you know, and it's not like you haven't been sick before."

"Uh-huh."

"Oh, Minerva. Grow up."

"Bye, Vienna. Thanks for calling."

Minerva hangs up without waiting for an answer.

She knows where she's seen her young mother's expression before. She feels her face pull into it when someone asks about the fiancé she's left behind.

Minerva goes to bed early every night, but her headaches only worsen as the time she spends at home increases. Alex has not contacted her and she had never given Anaïs her number; they had always seemed to know where to find one another.

Just the garden has faded. The flowerbeds are overgrown and Chris only shakes his head as he goes about his work.

"It's a damn shame, Minerva," he says one day when Minerva goes outside to help him. "All those lovely plants, gone. Maybe it's a curse? Did you anger anyone before you surprised us with a visit?"

Minerva ducks her head with a smile and pulls up another thistle. "Will these bulbs survive?"

"This season, sure, but I don't know about the next. For all we know, rabbits could dig 'em up in the mean time and have a feast." Chris takes off his battered hat and wipes his forehead. "Don't suppose you have any ideas?"

Minerva shakes her head, resting her dirty gloves on her jeans. "I'm having the same problem. Alex wanted to buy weed killer."

Chris scoffs. "And kill all the grass? Hardly worth the price of the weed killer unless you'd like a polka dot backyard."

"That's what I told him."

"You tried digging them up, I suppose?"

"No luck."

Something flickers in the corner of Minerva's vision and she jumps to her feet, spinning around. There's nothing but blue skies and the winding deer-beaten trails between the trees staring back.

"Minerva? Is something the matter?"

"No, it's nothing. I don't suppose you see anything strange out here?"

"Strange? I see lots of strange things. Mostly due to the trees—forests like this, they make people see things." He pulls a thistle from the garden. "Sometimes I think I see my late wife out here, wandering among the plants like she used to. But that's just nonsense; she's passed on and all the better for it."

"Just your wife?"

Chris shakes his head. "Memory's a powerful thing, Minerva. It'll let you remember happy times, but you've got to remember that the bad stuff will haunt you too."

Minerva looks towards the forest again and catches a glimpse of a small, laughing girl, running barefoot between the trees.

There's a porch swing that's swung empty since Minerva left. The wood is weathered with winter and memories, but her covered skin muffles them. She thinks of Anaïs, small apartment crowded with a ghost, and touches one finger cautiously to the wood.

Who do you shut out. Who do you keep.

The memories are faded, sepia photographs and speak softly to her. She and Vienna, rocking quietly in the fading evening. Minerva crying by herself, hours after her mother's funeral. Vienna's first love. Secret meetings on the porch when their father was out. Minerva and Laura, and feelings she didn't want to recognize. Boyfriends, breakups, Vienna leaving, Minerva's last night at home.

They're soft around the edges, muted.

Minerva swings and the swing creaks out a grainy rhythm.

It is a few hours past midnight when Minerva is shaken from her latest dizzying dream by the soft chimes on her cell phone. She fumbles for it in the darkness and finds a text message waiting for her.

I know it's late. I can't sleep. Your mom's gone. When are you coming back?

Minerva rests her cheek on her hand and stares at the message from Alex. She wonders what Vienna would say. "You both screwed up, call it even"? Minerva wonders if her mother will come back if she returns to Alex. She hasn't seen her at all since she's been back.

She looks at her cellphone again before putting it on the bedside table. It casts a ghostly hue on her ceiling, then flickers and goes out.

Minerva closes her eyes and waits for morning.

"Mail for you," her father greets when she walks into the kitchen for lunch. He points at a small envelope addressed to her in handwriting she doesn't recognize.

Minerva goes back to the porch swing and opens it.

Minerva,

I saw myself writing you this letter not long after you left and sent it to this address. So, when I recovered myself and cleaned up the coffee grounds I threw over the floor, I wrote a letter and sent it to this address because I already had written it in the future and I have to write it so

I have the vision in the past or else I'll never have sent a letter in the future.

(Don't think about it too hard. Trust me.)

Future me says, "Mausoleum." I have no idea what it means. Neither does future me.

—A

There's no return address.

Minerva stuffs the note into her pocket.

≈

Her cellphone rumbles this time, the only movement in the house, and Minerva wakes.

I'm sorry. Please come home so we can talk about it. Have been staying home every night after work. Miss you.

Minerva groans when she sees the time. Just after two.

The house sighs and mutters around her, restless.

Downstairs, Minerva hears an unfamiliar noise. She sits up slowly, freeing both ears. Minerva hears it again. She swings her legs over the side of the bed, finds her slippers and robe, and creeps down the dark hallway to the staircase.

There's a low glow coming from the kitchen. Minerva tiptoes through the puddles of moonlight slipping in through the cracks in curtains or shutters and skirts the cold spots lingering in the

73

hallways. The kitchen light is on when she reaches the ground floor. Minerva edges near the doorway and peers around the corner.

Her father is slumped forward, mumbling, and a bottle of antigeists is upended on the table before him. Her mother is standing on the other side of the table, staring down at him. She's different from when Minerva had seen her before, a twisted flesh-memory of who she once was: pallid skin and stains down the front of her nightgown. Her milky eyes drift up to meet Minerva's clear ones and she pulls back cracked lips to flash Minerva dirty, decaying teeth.

False, she says and flickers between the horrible specter and the pale, unhappy apparition that turned up at home.

With a jolt, she knows what Anaïs's letter meant.

"Dad."

"Minnie, what are you doing up?" her father hisses. "Go back to bed *this instant*."

"How long have you been seeing her?"

"What? What on earth are you talking about?"

"Can't you hear her? She's trying to tell us something."

"Minerva, she's just a ghost. She means nothing." But her father's eyes are bloodshot, and the bruises under his eyes match Minerva's own insomnia.

"What did you do with her remains?"

"Minerva—"

"If there's any way to put her to rest—"

"We've already done it, Minerva! We can't do anything else but *forget* and move on with our lives. Your mother made the decision to leave and she looked without leaping. Like she always did."

Minerva's mother hangs back, suspended like a puppet on tangled strings.

"How long have you been seeing her?"

Her father is quiet for a moment and when he speaks again, his voice is choked. "Years, but not consistently." He laughs. "She comes and goes as she pleases, just like she always did. Not very responsible, your mother. Not cut out to raise two girls, especially with one who isn't much interested in tradition or following a set path."

"Suppose I get that from her."

Minerva's mother slips backwards and disappears into the pantry.

"I'm going to bed and you should, too. If you want to pay your respects to your mother, do it in the morning at the family's mausoleum, but don't mention her again. Do you understand?"

Minerva says nothing and retreats.

"Ideali-Tea, Coffee and Teas, how may I help you?"

"Anaïs?"

"Yes?"

"It's Minerva."

"How did you get this number?"

"It's in the phonebook."

"Oh."

"I think I know what I have to do."

Anaïs cradles the phone between her shoulder and ear as she rings up a customer. "Oh?"

"I got your note."

"I knew you would."

Minerva snorts out a laugh on the other end and despite herself, Anaïs feels herself smiling.

"Do you see if I'm coming back?"

"No idea. I don't choose the visions, you know."

"Hm."

"Your future is still relative, I guess."

"Is that a good thing?"

"It's the best thing. Take it from me. I'm an expert."

"Even with seeing your own death?"

"Jury's still out."

"Maybe I'll see you."

"Maybe you won't."

They hang up.

Anaïs turns her head and sees the young girl in the corner, still reading. She watches her for a long time until the chime above the door breaks her daydream. Anaïs smiles and turns to help the customer. When she looks back, the girl is gone.

When Minerva returns to her room, she begins packing and leaves with the sunrise. The caretaker lets her into the cemetery and out again.

"I'm moving my flight up," she tells her father when he calls to ask where she is. "I'm sorry I left without saying goodbye."

"It's all right, pumpkin," he answers wearily. "I'll see you in a few months for the wedding."

Minerva takes the next flight out and returns home to a sunny afternoon. She rents a car, driving past where she and Alex live and into the sprawling country that lies beyond. It is here that her mother grew up. The affluence had dulled her brightness, left her trapped and feeling like little more than an exhibit.

Minerva's father had tried, even after Minerva's mother had passed, but an urn engraved with a thistle design was not the same as her ashes being scattered as her mother had wished. Minerva's mother never wanted to be a fading memory, shelved and gathering dust. She never wanted to be pulled back, a specter of herself.

Minerva supposes the dilution of distance, the guilt instead of anger, was what had smoothed out her mother's appearance.

Compromise. Not sacrifice.

VII

Minerva pulls down a dirt road until she reaches a small grove of trees edging a crisp, blue lake. She's been here once or twice when school holidays would allow it. Loving nature was genetic, she supposed, and Minerva was more like her mother than Vienna. And so, it is here that Minerva knows her mother grew up, fell in love, and wished to return.

Minerva walks to the lake's edge and pulls out the bag containing her mother's ashes. She wonders how long it will take someone to notice she's left a bag of dirt, dug from the thistle-flooded garden, in their place. Never, she decides.

Minerva takes a deep breath, holds it, and upends the bag, scattering it into the wind and over the lake. She stays there for a long time, breathing easily in the clean air and underneath a wide-arching sky.

When she returns to her rental car, she finds two people waiting. Ghosts, she knows, even before the tingles start; they're not substantial enough to be real.

Alex gives her a shy, charming smile. Anaïs is grinning, leaning back comfortably against Minerva's car, like she's part of it, like she fits.

Time to come home.

Minerva watches both of them until they fade. Time to choose.

Her engagement ring is a solitaire sapphire. She told Alex she didn't like diamonds, preferred other stones. It wasn't a lie; sapphires are quieter gems.

There's a letter on the counter. This time she recognizes the handwriting. When Minerva opens it, there are only two lines.

I lied. Good luck.
      —A

She leaves ring and house key on the kitchen counter and nothing in the drawers of her dresser.

Emily Capettini holds a Ph.D. in English from the University of Louisiana at Lafayette and works as an Assistant Editor. Her fiction has previously appeared in *The Battered Suitcase, The Louisiana Review, Stone Highway Review, Noctua Review, The Future Fire: Outlaw Bodies Anthology, Stirring: A Literary Collection,* and *Not Somewhere Else But Here: A Contemporary Anthology of Women and Place* (Sundress Publications, 2013). Her critical work has appeared in *Feminism in the Worlds of Neil Gaiman: Essays on the Comics, Poetry, and Prose* (McFarland & Company, 2012) and *Neil Gaiman in the 21st Century: Essays on the Novels, Children's Stories, Online Writings, Comics and Other Works* (McFarland & Company, 2015). She received her B.A. in English and French from Lake Forest College in 2009. In her free time, Emily runs, bakes, and blogs about women and *Doctor Who*. She lives in Maryland.

Thistle
by Emily Capettini

Cover text set in Lithos Pro & Kabel Lt. Std
Interior text set in Adobe Garamond Pro, Lithos Pro & Kabel Lt. Std.

Cover Photo © Copyright Corbis/42-30533422 Thistle head

Cover and interior design by Ken Keegan

Omnidawn Publishing
Oakland, California
2015
Rusty Morrison & Ken Keegan, senior editors & co-publishers
Gillian Olivia Blythe Hamel, managing editor
Cassandra Smith, poetry editor & book designer
Peter Burghardt, poetry editor & book designer
Melissa Burke, poetry editor & marketing manager
Sharon Zetter, poetry editor, book designer, & grant writer
Liza Flum, poetry editor
RJ Ingram, poetry editor
Juliana Paslay, fiction editor
Gail Aronson, fiction editor
Josie Gallup, publicity assistant
Sheila Sumner, publicity assistant
Kevin Peters, warehouse manager
Janelle Bonifacio, office assistant
Abbigail Baldys, administrative assistant